Clark in the
DEEP SEA

R. W. Alley

CLARION BOOKS
Houghton Mifflin Harcourt
Boston • New York

Clarion Books ◆ 215 Park Avenue South ◆ New York, New York 10003
Copyright © 2016 by R.W. Alley ◆ All rights reserved. For information about
permission to reproduce selections from this book, write to Permissions, Houghton Mifflin
Harcourt Publishing Company, 215 Park Avenue South, New York, New York 10003.
Clarion Books is an imprint of Houghton Mifflin Harcourt Publishing Company. ◆ www.hmhco.com
The illustrations in this book were done in ink, pencils, watercolors, gouaches, and acrylics on
Bristol board paper. ◆ The text was set in Julius Primary.
Library of Congress Cataloging-in-Publication Data is available.
ISBN 978-0-547-90692-8
Manufactured in Malaysia   TWP 10 9 8 7 6 5 4 3 2 1   4500562707

With love to Z & C & M for making my world so colorful

ONE soggy spring day,
Clark was busy coloring
when Gretchen announced,
"It's circus time!"

"Presenting Bear-O the Balancing Bear
with the famous Roly-Poly People!"
But Bear forgot to balance.

"Bear overboard," said Annabelle.
"Launch the lifeboats!" called Mitchell.
"No time!" cried Clark. "I'll save Bear!"
Fearlessly, he leaped over the side...

...and into his
deep-sea gear.

What's this? Horrors!
It's a rare, hungry Fur-Shark.
"Un-mouth that bear!"
ordered Clark.

Bravely, Clark tickle-tussled the
Fur-Shark until...
POP! Bear floated free!
"Hooray!" said Bear.

But—double horrors!
The sea swept him
into the Fur-Shark's
ghastly, dark cave.
"Yuck," said Bear.

The cave reeked. It stank.
But Clark had a job to do.
"I'm coming, Bear!" he called.

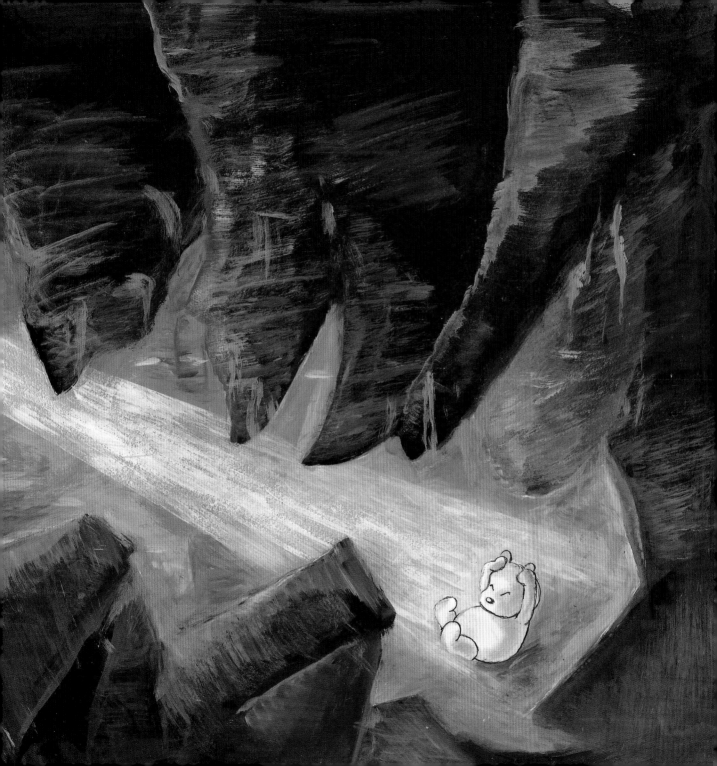

Clark grabbed Bear and swam up and up.
"Be brave," he told Bear.
"I'll try," said Bear.

Suddenly...

Triple horrors!

The Million-Mile Eel
trapped Clark by the fins!

SWIZZZ came the eel's icy spray,
pushing Clark and Bear
into the seaweed bog.

"We're stuck!" shouted Clark.
"And our air is low. What a way to go!"
But then…

Sea Patrol arrived!
They steered their submarine
to the rescue.

First Sea Patrol unstuck Clark.
Then Clark unstuck Bear.
"Ouch!" A little fur pulled off.

"You were very brave," said Clark.
"You were too," said Bear.

They were headed for home
when the sea got wild.
"Abandon ship!" shouted Clark.

"Hooray!"
said Gretchen.

Safe from the sea,
everyone dried off
and waited for the rain to stop.